Ken Read celebrates his victory at Val-d'Isère

Klammer hadn't fallen. When Klammer won the next race five days later, everything seemed to be back to normal. "I know I can win every other race this season," Klammer said.

A French poster marking his win at Val-d'Isère says:
"Ken Read flies to victory."

Still, it was another good day for the Canadians. All five of them finished close behind Klammer. "My biggest threat will come from the Canadians," he admitted. He was right.

In the very next race, at Schladming, Austria, a Canadian won again. This time it was Dave Irwin. He finished nearly two seconds faster than anyone else. "I told you the Canadians would win more races," said Ir with a big smile. No one could say Ken's win was a fluke now. Everything was starting to fall into place.

5 Skiing Like Crazy

It was December 1975 when talk of "the Crazy Canucks" first began. Serge Lang was probably the man who started it. Serge was a French reporter who had created the World Cup back in 1966. After Ken won, he wrote: "These Canucks ski like they're crazy ... taking every risk." Swiss skier Philippe Roux said something very similar after Ir's victory: "Irwin and his teammates ski with fantastic daring. They're crazy, these Canadians."

Serge Lang appreciated what the Canadian ski team had done. As the founder of the World Cup, he wanted to see Canada succeed. It would be good for business. He knew that a strong Canadian team would attract new fans in Canada and the United States. Not many other European journalists cared about that. They still saw downhill ski racing as their sport. When they called the Canadians "Crazy Canucks," they meant it as an insult. Skiers from Switzerland and Austria had been the best for years. They couldn't believe that Canadian skiers could keep up with them. When Franz Klammer took big risks, they called him a great champion. When the Canadian team took the same risks, they called them crazy.

Eventually, the name Crazy Canucks became something to be proud of. Fans in Europe came to love the team's wild style. Canadians were slower to catch on. But when they did, they were proud of the way their daredevil skiers beat the Europeans at their own game. It was true that the Crazy Canucks took a lot of chances. They felt they had to. It wasn't because they were crazy. They just wanted to find out for themselves what they could and couldn't do on the mountains. They didn't want to take anyone else's word for it. So, they raced all-out, all the time, even in their training runs. They tucked where other people said they shouldn't. They tried to make turns without slowing down. Sometimes they crashed, but they didn't see it as being reckless. They were just looking for ways to shave a few seconds off their time.

"We took risks," Ken admitted. "But they were calculated risks. We took chances others weren't willing to take."

"They called us crazy," Steve said, "but really, we were just doing things they thought we couldn't do."

Both Ken and Steve truly believed it was more dangerous to drive a car on the highway than it was for a well-trained skier to race in a downhill. Sometimes, though, the results on the hill were pretty scary, like at Wengen, Switzerland. It was a few weeks after Ir's win at Schladming. Both Ken and Ir crashed. Ken was all right, but Ir was not. He was really attacking the hill when he spun off a bump. A gust of wind caught him and twisted him further around. "This is gonna be a good one," he thought, as he cartwheeled off a steep slope. He had been going about 120 kilometres an hour when he crashed. The blow to his head when he landed knocked him unconscious.

Ken had fallen in nearly the same place. He saw what happened to Ir, and radioed the results to his teammates: "Ir's skis and equipment are destroyed." His glasses were broken too, and the pieces had cut his face. "His goggles are filled with blood." The crash looked so scary that a Swiss company later used a video of it to sell life insurance!

Ir had suffered a serious concussion. He had also broken a couple of ribs. Amazingly, he was back in action less than a month later. He kept pushing himself hard after his crash. He still had some great races, but he was never really the same skier. He got injured a lot.

A few weeks after the crash, the World Cup circuit had a break in its schedule. The break let the World Cup skiers race at the 1976 Winter Olympics. Ir made it back in time for the Olympic Games, but Steve didn't. He had crashed while going all-out in a training run at Kitzbuhel. Instead of going to Innsbruck for the Olympics, Steve went home to Toronto. He needed major surgery on his right knee. While his teammates trained for the big race, Steve lay in bed with a large cast on his leg.

Steve knew it would take a lot of hard work to get back in shape for the World Cup. Watching the Olympics helped to inspire him. Franz Klammer skied a fantastic race. He flew down the mountain, barely under control, to beat Bernhard Russi for the gold medal. The

Ken Read, Jim Hunter, Dave Irwin, and Dave Murray at the 1976 Winter Olympics in Innsbruck, Austria

Crazy Canucks did pretty well too. Ken finished fifth. Ir was eighth, and Jim was tenth.

Despite the crashes, the 1975–76 season was a success for the Canadians.

But the winter of 1976–77 would prove to be a disaster.

6 Changing with the Times

Steve was healthy again by the winter of 1976–77. Still, he called that year "Hell Season." He said it was, "The worst time of my life, much worse than my knee injuries."

The whole team struggled that winter. No one finished higher than 13th all year. Since his crash, Ir had been having problems with his vision and his memory. Jim was getting burned out by all the bad results. Scott's answer was to work the team harder than ever. This was starting to become a problem. The skiers didn't need more work. They needed better equipment. Scott was not keeping up with the latest technology. There were problems with the skis. There were problems with the wax. The worst problems were with the downhill suits. The Canadian skiers were sure their suits were slowing them down. They felt they were letting too much air get in, but no one seemed to believe them.

After the season, the Crazy Canucks had their downhill suits tested at the National Research Centre in Ottawa. The tests proved that the skiers were right. Their suits did let too much air in. It was as if they had been wearing little parachutes. No wonder their times had been so slow! It would have been nearly impossible to win wearing those downhill suits.

In 1977–78, the team got new downhill

suits, the same as the ones the Austrians had been wearing. There were lots of other changes too. Jim decided to leave the team. He wasn't happy focusing on the downhill. Ken, Steve, Ir, and Mur were the only ones left. They became the Crazy Canucks everyone would remember.

There was a new coach that year too. John Ritchie was put in charge, and got an assistant to specialize as a downhill coach. He was a former Swiss skier named Heinz Kappeler. John Ritchie was a change from Scott Henderson. He made sure everyone on the team had a say in how decisions got made. He worked behind the scenes to make things better for the skiers, while Heinz did most of the work on the hill with them.

The team had a new serviceman too. Hans Rammelmueller now looked after the skis and wax. Hans was their third serviceman, and their best by far. He was an Austrian, so it was easier for him to get along with the Fischer Ski people. That had been a problem for the Canadian Hans replaced.

Despite all the changes, one important thing remained the same. Teamwork was just as important as ever. "We all want to show the Europeans that we can ski with the best," Ken said. "We've solved our technical problems. We've got an open-minded coach. We're ready."

People had begun to think of Ken as the leader of the Crazy Canucks. He was handsome and he was smart. He always gave thoughtful answers when reporters asked him questions. He loved travelling in Europe, and he was the first Canadian to master other languages. Most importantly, he was also the team's top skier!

Midway through the 1977–78 season, Ken got Canada back on the winner's podium. It was the team's first win in

Ken Read speaking to the press

almost two years. Dave Murray was second that day. That was Mur's best finish so far in his World Cup career. When the season ended, Ken was ranked fourth in the world in the downhill standings. Mur was 12th and Steve was 15th.

All in all, it had been a very good year, but the European press still didn't show the team any respect. The fact book for the World Cup tour was 120 pages long, but Ken and Mur's 1–2 finish got only a single sentence! And the sentence wasn't very flattering. It said the Canadians won because the other skiers had relaxed too much after finishing a more important race.

The European media may not have liked the Canadian team, but the fans were starting to. Ken, Steve, Mur, and Ir could all speak several languages by that time. They were always open and friendly with fans wherever they went. Soon, it seemed the Crazy Canucks were everybody's second-favourite team. Swiss fans would say, "If we can't win, we sure hope one of you beats the Austrians." Austrian fans would say the same thing about the Canadians and the Swiss. These were good times for the Canadian ski team. Yet there were still a few bumps in the road.

7 Struggling to Fit In

Warm weather at Val-d'Isère in December of 1978 meant the 1978–79 ski season opened at Schladming. The Canadian team had brand new Austrian downhill suits to start the winter. The suits met all the proper air standards ... but the fit was horrible! So, just before the first race, the Canadians switched to Italian suits. These suits were thinner and the fit was a lot more snug. Skiing in his new red suit, Ken won two of the four training runs. The Austrian newspapers weren't impressed. Now they started calling the Canadians "world training champions."

There had not been a World Cup race at Schladming since Ir won there in 1975. The course was very fast. It had lots of steep drops, and only a few jumps. Unlike Kitzbuhel, Schladming was very wide, so the turns were not so tough. "It's like driving down a six-lane highway," Steve said. "Not like a twisting mountain road."

The course was very icy in training. Then, on race day, a warm wind threatened to turn the snow to mush. It turned out be much faster than it looked. Ken was able to blaze down very quickly. In the finish area, he got on the walkie-talkie. "The snow is grippier than in training," Ken told his teammates. "But you can run it pretty much the same."

Ken knew he had a fast time, but there

were still lots of racers left to ski. Yet, as each new time flashed on the scoreboard, none of the Europeans matched him. Then it was Mur's turn. He flew down the mountain just like Ken had told him to. He was on pace with Ken the whole way down. When Mur skied across the finish line, his time flashed on the board. It was good enough for second place. It was another 1–2 finish for Ken and Mur!

When the trophies were handed out, Mur looked up at Ken from the second-place podium. "What do I have to do to beat you, Read?" he said with a smile. Ken smiled back. "Ski a little faster!" he answered. But both racers knew it really didn't matter which of them had won. The important thing was that two Canadians finished on top. Making the day even better, Ir finished seventh in the race and Steve was ninth. It was the best showing yet by the Crazy Canucks.

Ken Read and Steve Podborski celebrate after a successful race

Ken was a perfectionist. Despite his win, he still wasn't happy with his downhill suit. In January 1979, a Japanese company designed new suits especially for

Athlete of the Year

When the Crazy Canucks struggled, they were usually ignored by the newspapers at home. But when the wins began piling up, Canadians really started taking an interest. Proof of that came in December of 1978. Ken Read finished tied for first place in the vote for Canada's top athlete. Ken shared the Lou Marsh Trophy with swimmer Graham Smith.

the Canadian team. The suits were lemon yellow, but they had a bright red maple leaf just below each shoulder. They were given to the team just before a race in Morzine, France. The Canadians agreed to try them right away. "Mine was perfect," Ken said. "Never in my life had I put on such a snug suit."

There was just one problem. The World Cup organizers had not approved the new suits. But they were made out of the same material as the downhill suits the Swiss team was using. The Japanese team was going to wear them. So were the skiers from Australia.

Steve decided he didn't want to race in a suit he'd never trained in. He wore his old suit. Ken and Mur wore the new ones. (Ir had been injured again, and wasn't

Dave Murray in action after the team switched to yellow racing suits

racing that weekend.)

The Morzine course was short, but tricky. A racer had to have his wits about him the whole time. There were lots of tough turns in the upper section. If a racer messed up in the lengthy bends or the tricky S-turns, he wouldn't be able to go fast enough for the straight run to the finish. Steve was the first racer down the hill that day. Even in his old suit, he skied brilliantly. He made one small mistake on a turn near the top, but he was fine after that.

"Boy, it was fast," Steve said. "I took off at a bump halfway down the course and really flew. I must have earned my pilot's licence."

Then it was Steve's turn to wait. Through the first 13 racers, no one came close to him. Ken was racer number 14. He was flying too. He made a small mistake near the middle of the mountain, but he recovered quickly. When he crossed the finish line, Ken was nearly a half-second faster than Steve. It was another 1–2 finish for the Crazy Canucks! Herbert Plank of Italy finished third.

After the race, the Italian team filed a protest. They wanted Ken's new suit to be tested. The Canadians had known that this might happen, but they weren't worried. Even a World Cup official said he thought Ken's suit would pass the test. But it didn't. There had been a mistake in the fabric. The suit didn't let enough air get through. Ken was disqualified. Steve was awarded his first World Cup victory. This was not the way he had hoped he would win his first race. He would never see it as a true victory. Even the Austrians believed that Ken deserved the win. "The suit didn't matter," said the Austrian coach. "He would have won if he raced in a business suit."

Later tests showed that Ken's suit was

actually fine. The Canadian team filed a protest, but Ken never got the win back. A season that had started so well began to fall apart. There were still some good results, but nothing seemed to go Canada's way. Even a race scheduled for Whistler Mountain in British Columbia had to be cancelled when the weather turned warm. The Europeans claimed it made racing too dangerous.

The race at Whistler would have been the Crazy Canucks' first chance to ski a World Cup race in their home country. They were very angry when it was cancelled. Mur was particularly upset. He was from Whistler, and he had just finished third in a race one week earlier. The Canadians all felt the race could have been run, and that Europeans just didn't want to race in Canada.

Instead of holding a real World Cup downhill, the skiers held an exhibition race at Whistler. At least the growing number of fans in Canada would get something to watch. Extra turn gates were placed on the course to slow everybody down. Ken decided to ignore them. He skied like it was a true downhill race. He did it to send a message to the Europeans: There is nothing wrong with this Canadian mountain, and there is nothing wrong with Canada's ski team.

8 Conquering at Kitzbuhel

The 1978–79 season had actually been another good one for the Crazy Canucks. Steve and Mur were tied for tenth in the downhill standings. Ken finished fourth for the second year in a row. With the 25 extra points he should have had at Morzine, and with a chance to race at Whistler, he might have finished first. Instead, a Swiss skier became the new World Cup champion. Peter Mueller was now the racer everyone else was gunning for. The Canadians felt they were ready to challenge him in 1979–80.

"There are 15 skiers in the world today who can win a World Cup or Olympic race," said Canadian coach John Ritchie in December 1979. "We have four of them."

John believed there was only one reason that the Swiss and Austrians were still doing better than the Canadians. The Europeans were competing at home. "We have to live, eat, and sleep in their environment for months on end. For that reason, I feel we really have the best downhillers in the world."

Come February 1980, the Europeans would get a taste of their own medicine. The World Cup season was going to end early in Europe. After that, the Winter Olympics would be held in North America — not in Canada, but at Lake Placid in the United States.

The Canadian team was excited to

begin the 1979–80 season, but it got off to a bad start. In the first race at Val-d'Isère, Mur was ninth and Ir was fourteenth. At least they finished the race. Ken and Steve both crashed. They fell in almost the same place on the course. Only a safety net at the side of the hill saved them from serious injuries.

Things got even worse the next week. Ken had been the fastest by far in the training runs. Then, the night before the race, he drew the number-one start position, and it snowed. Ken's time in the race was nearly three seconds slower than his best training run. He finished in seventh place. Mur was 11th, but Steve finished 45th. He hadn't done that badly in years! "I was embarrassed," Steve said. "It was absolutely ridiculous." Ir did even worse. He was 56th. Something had gone wrong. But what?

The Canadians found out a few days

later. The Fischer Ski Company had come up with a brand new wax. They wanted to use it right away. Hans, who took care of the Canadian skis, didn't want to use the wax without testing it first. The Fischer people told him he had to. So he spread it on the bottom of the Canadian skis. Obviously, the wax didn't work. "It was like glue," Ken said. Peter Mueller didn't use Fischer skis, so he didn't have the new wax. Mueller wound up winning the race ... but his time was two seconds slower than Ken's best time in training.

The next week at Schladming, everything finally seemed to be right ... except for the weather. The race started in a slight drizzle of rain. Soon, it was raining harder. Both Ken and Steve had early start numbers, and both had blazed down the mountain. Through the first 26 racers, Steve had the best time. Ken was third. There were still 44 racers to go, but all the

Ski Wax

Ski wax is a special material applied to the bottom of skis. Wax helps to reduce friction between the skis and the snow and lets the skis glide quickly. There are many types of ski wax, and they work differently in different weather conditions. Using the right wax at the right time can make a big difference to a ski racer.

best skiers had already come down. There was no way anyone else would be able to beat them. But when it started to rain hard, the World Cup officials called off the race. Steve got to keep his victory trophy, but the points he and Ken should have earned wouldn't count in the standings.

It was yet another disappointment. But, "around here," John reminded them, "it's not how many times you get knocked down. It's how fast you get up." So, the Canadian team went home for Christmas and tried to forget their troubles. They knew they would have to do better in the New Year. And they did. Things finally started to turn around on January 12, 1980, the day that Ken won the annual Hahnenkamm race in Kitzbuhel.

There wasn't a better place for Ken to win. Downhill races had been held in the town of Kitzbuhel since 1905. The Hahnenkamm race had begun in 1931, and the steep Streif course had been used since the 1940s. Kitzbuhel's long history was the main reason the race was so important. The fact that Austrians took their racing so seriously added to the drama. Even the town itself made the race more exciting. Kitzbuhel looked like something out of a fairy tale. It was built high up in the mountains, with castles all around the area. The finish line for the race was practically in the centre of town.

In the three training runs leading up to

the race, Steve had won the first one and Ken had won the second. Of course, good training runs didn't always mean good races. So far that season, a Canadian had finished first in training eight times. Once again newspapers in Europe were making fun of the team as the "world training champions."

When Ken conquered Kitzbuhel that day, it was the biggest victory of his career. He spent hours after the race giving interviews in English, French, and German. Then, there were the parties. Everyone wanted to toast Ken's success. Everywhere he went that night, there was clapping and singing and champagne corks popping. It was all a lot of fun. It was also a great way to forget the struggles of the early season.

With the Olympics only a month away, Ken knew he was peaking at just the right time. Everyone started saying he would be

Ken Read received this unusual trophy for winning the Hahnenkamm, which means "rooster comb" in German. The shape of the mountain is similar to the spiky crown on top of a rooster's head.

the favourite for the gold medal. Ken couldn't worry about that yet. There were other things to focus on first, like trying to win the World Cup title.

A week after Kitzbuhel, the World Cup moved on to another famous old race: the Lauberhorn in Wengen, Switzerland. Wengen is on one of the most beautiful mountains in Europe. But there wasn't much time to enjoy the scenery. The course demanded total concentration. It was 4.5 kilometres long, the longest race on the World Cup. With lots of tight turns near the bottom, it felt even longer than it was. "Calves, thighs, and hearts scream for rest," Ken said. "Those extra 30 seconds put racers at risk for disaster." Wengen was where Ir had crashed back in 1976. There were many dangerous sections to watch out for. "Half the time," said Steve, "it's like falling down an elevator shaft."

Two races were scheduled for Wengen to make up for the rainout at Schladming. During training, downhill coach Heinz came up with a daring plan. At Kitzbuhel, he'd been the one who told Ken to turn early when he saw the fence. His new plan was exactly the opposite. Heinz noticed that most racers were slowing down before the tight turns at the bottom of the Wengen course. He told the Canadians to stay in their tucks until the last possible moment and take the turns fast. Heinz wanted them to lean right into the gates, as if they were racing in a giant slalom. A move like that takes lots of courage ... but the Crazy Canucks were never ones to back down from a challenge!

Ken started slowly in the first race, but he picked up speed as he went along. When he neared the bottom, he went as fast as he could into the turns. Then, he dug in hard with the edges of his skis, slowing down just enough to twist around the gates. He barely lost any speed as he flew towards the finish. When he crossed the line, the fans went crazy.

Ken not only won the race, he skied the long course faster than anyone ever had before. But Ken's new record didn't last long. Steve skied even faster the next day. He wasn't fast enough to win, though. Ken then broke that record on his next run.

Unfortunately for the two Canadians, neither of them were fast enough in the end. Peter Mueller beat them both. The Swiss ace finished first, with Ken second and Steve third.

Mueller's win at Wengen was his third of the season. He was on top in the World Cup standings, but Ken had moved into a close second. Ken still studied the World Cup points carefully, so he knew exactly what he had to do. To have any chance at the title, he had to finish first or second in the final race.

The odds were in Mueller's favour, but Ken was skiing much better than he had been in training for the last race. He broke the course record by four seconds in his final run. Everything was looking good … until the weather changed. It went from cold and clear to warm and foggy. It was impossible to see the course, so the race had to be cancelled.

For a while, it looked like Mueller would win the title by default. Later, World Cup officials decided to hold a makeup race. It would be run after the Olympics. And, it would be held at Lake Louise — in Canada. Ken would be racing on his "home" course!

World Cup Scoring

During the time of the Crazy Canucks, the top 15 finishers in each World Cup race were awarded points. These points were used to determine the World Cup champion. The winner of each race got 25 points. Second place got 20 points. Third place got 15 points, and fourth place got 12. After that, points dropped off from 11 to 1 for the racers who finish fifth to 15th. At the end of the season, skiers counted the points they earned in their five best races. Whoever had the most points was the World Cup champion.

9 Olympic Expectations

Sometimes, when the Crazy Canucks came home from Europe, there were a few fans waiting for them at the airport. Sometimes there were a few reporters too. Usually they were junior reporters. Very few of the major sportswriters paid much attention to ski racing.

All that changed when the team came home before the 1980 Winter Olympics. Their recent success fuelled excitement about the Olympics. Suddenly it seemed everyone in Canada had become a ski fan. All the newspapers wanted stories.

When their plane landed in Toronto, the Crazy Canucks collected their luggage and equipment. They loaded everything onto trolleys. They pushed them through Customs, just like they always did. When they got out, they found themselves in a huge mob of fans. They were led through the crowd to a small room that was packed with journalists. There, they sat and answered questions … until it was time to get on the next plane for Calgary. Then, the same thing happened all over again. Calgary was Ken's hometown. One of the fans in the airport there had a sign that said, "*Ken Read for Prime Minister.*"

Ken had a few days to relax at home. To stay in shape, he went skiing at Lake Louise. He didn't want to lose the perfect flow he had felt in the recent races. After a few days in the Canadian Rockies, Ken flew to Quebec City. The Crazy Canucks were going to hold a mini Olympic training camp at nearby Mont-Sainte-Anne. It would be a good test for them. The hills and snow were very similar to what they would race on at Lake Placid.

Like the airports, Mont-Sainte-Anne was filled with reporters. The Canadian Ski Association arranged for dozens of interviews. They also set up a lot of parties for the team's sponsors to meet the team. The skiers knew these events were important. The team was always short on money, and this would help a lot. Even so, they started to wonder if they were getting in enough training. Their final runs were even cut short so they could drive to Montreal for more parties.

On February 8, 1980, the team arrived in Lake Placid. They had come early to continue their training. If they thought things would be better in Lake Placid, they were wrong. The Crazy Canucks had never been in such a big race so close to home. Everyone wanted a part of them. There was more media in Lake Placid than they had ever seen. As soon as the Canadians got to the Olympic Village, reporters began waving microphones in their faces. Cameramen followed them as they went inside. One of them asked Ken to pose for a picture opening the door to his room. Another followed Steve right inside his room to take more pictures.

After the team got settled in, the Canadian Olympic Association started shuffling the Crazy Canucks to party after party. Everyone wanted the skiers to say that Ken was going to win a gold medal. Many people reported that any three of the four Crazy Canucks could sweep all three downhill medals. The skiers refused to make predictions. "We tried to explain it to them," Steve said. "There were about

Money Matters

In the days of the Crazy Canucks, Olympic athletes had to be amateurs. However, many ski racers earned lots of money. To be eligible for the Olympics, the skiers wouldn't get their money until they retired. In the beginning, the Crazy Canucks were lucky to earn a few thousand dollars per year. Later, their ski companies paid them up to $50,000 per win. Other sponsors paid them too. A lot of the sponsorship money went straight to the Canadian Ski Association, which paid for most of the team's training costs.

a hundred of the best skiers in the world standing between us and the medals." The Crazy Canucks knew much better than the reporters that anything could happen on the day of a race.

Training runs for the downhill started before the Olympics even began. The Canadians didn't do as well as they had hoped. Finally, on the last day, their times started to improve. Ken felt that if he improved by the same amount in the real race, he could win the Olympic downhill. After the last training run, he got to carry the flag for Canada in the opening ceremonies. Ken hoped he'd get to carry a gold medal the next day.

The Olympic downhill was scheduled for February 14. It was snowy and windy. At least all the Canadians had good start numbers. Mur was the first of them on the hill, but he didn't have a very good run. (He wound up in tenth place; Ir finished in 11th.) Everyone watching the race live on TV back home in Canada expected Ken to be much faster.

The top part of the Lake Placid course was flat. Instead of the usual three thrusts with his skis and poles, Ken pushed four times. Then he dropped into his tuck. The first turn was a sharp bend to the left. It

Queens of the Slopes

Before the Crazy Canucks, Canada's best skiers were all women. In 1956, Lucille Wheeler won a bronze medal in the Olympic downhill. In 1960, Ann Heggtveit won a gold medal in slalom. Nancy Greene won two medals in 1968. Even after the Crazy Canucks, Canadian women starred. Kathy Kreiner won Olympic gold in the giant slalom in 1976. Karen Percy won two bronze medals in 1988. Karen Lee-Gartner won downhill gold in 1992. And while neither Laurie Graham nor Gerry Sorenson ever won an Olympic medal, they won a combined total of 11 World Cup races.

was tricky, but Ken made it perfectly. He was right on line at the second turn and sped down a sharp drop. Next came four quick little bends. Ken leaned hard on his right ski and made the first bend just the way he wanted. Then he had to apply the right amount of pressure to change direction. When he shifted his weight to his left leg, he hit a small bump. His left foot bounced a tiny bit, and when it came back down, his ski popped off! Ken fell over and skidded to a stop.

Less than 15 seconds into his Olympic run, Ken's race was over. There would be no gold medal for him. No one ever figured out what made his ski come off. It was just more bad luck.

Steve was in the start hut when Ken had his mishap. He didn't hear about what had happened. Later, he said he was glad he didn't know. Steve had found all the parties and interviews troubling enough. Hearing about Ken would have only made things worse.

As the youngest member of the Canadian ski team, Steve had been behind the others in the early years. That was no longer true. He started having more and more success. Steve had always been smooth on his skis. He could make his turns faster than anyone else. Sometimes, like Ir, Steve was too fast for his own good. Often, he would either do well in a race or crash. Finally, he seemed to be getting everything under control.

After all the distractions leading up to the Olympics, Steve felt a huge sense of relief to finally be racing. Still, he had his own problem near the top of the course. "I came hard around a turn," he said after, "and nearly missed it." Steve was able to recover, but the snow and wind made it hard to see. It was almost impossible to spot the dangerous bumps. "I really got shaken up on the upper part," Steve admitted. "I gave up a little time there, but I think I regained it on the lower part."

Steve didn't run a perfect race, but it was good enough for third place. People

Steve Podborski shows his Olympic bronze medal to fans at the Craigleith ski club where his racing career began

were sad that Ken missed his chance for gold, but Steve won the bronze medal. He was the first male skier from Canada ever to win an Olympic medal.

10 Taking Aim at Top Spot

Ken was disappointed with what happened to him in Lake Placid. Winning an Olympic gold medal would have been a once-in-a-lifetime experience, something that no one would ever forget. Still, Ken knew the Olympics were really just one race. Winning the World Cup title would mean being the best downhill skier for an entire season. Ken still had a chance to do that.

The race at Lake Louise was held on

March 4, 1980. But Ken ran into more bad luck. He drew the fourth start position, which wasn't very good. When it snowed heavily before the race, Ken knew he had almost no chance at all. He finished in eighth place. Peter Mueller finished 14th, but it didn't matter. In the final standings, Mueller was the World Cup downhill champion. Ken came in second.

"You're always looking for the perfect run," Ken said. "But it never happens. Some people may say I choked. I don't think I did. I wound up second overall in the whole world. How many Canadians can make that claim?"

Ken's second-place finish in the World Cup standings was the best yet for the Crazy Canucks. Still, their goal was for one of them to finish first. Would Ken finally top the standings in 1980–81? Some people were starting to think that another Canadian might. Steve had come in fourth at Lake Louise, and finished ninth in the overall standings. Those results, plus his Olympic bronze medal, had many people thinking Steve was ready for a big breakthrough. Instead, he nearly had a major breakdown.

In May 1980, Steve and Ken were back in Europe. They were testing new skis on a glacier in Austria. The weather was warm and the snow was wet and heavy. As Steve lugged his long racing skis through a turn, he felt something pop in his right knee. It was the same knee that had needed surgery back in 1976. This time, the damage was much worse.

Steve had completely destroyed his knee. A cameraman who was supposed to film the operation had to walk out when he saw the damage. (He passed out in a bathroom!) "The ligaments looked like spaghetti in tomato sauce," Steve said. To fix it, a doctor had to take a piece of muscle out of Steve's thigh. Then he used the muscle to build new ligaments. The new pieces were sewn right through Steve's knee.

Steve had to spend the next five weeks in a cast. The cast went all the way from his hip to his toes. It finally came off in July. There was no way Steve was going to make the Crazy Canucks' South American training camp that summer. He would have to get ready on his own. No athlete had ever returned to the top of his sport after that type of operation. Steve was determined that he would. He rode his bike more than 300 kilometres every week to get strong again. He lifted weights, and worked with a trainer five days a week.

Finally, by the end of October, Steve was back on his skis. All the hard work had made him hungrier than ever for success. Still, no one knew how his knee would hold up to World Cup competition. With ten races now on the schedule, the 1980–81 season was going to be the longest ever. As usual, it began in Val-d'Isère on the first weekend in December.

Steve was not very happy when he saw the video of his training runs. "I was skiing like my grandmother," he said. But the results of his hard work were better than they looked. His times were getting faster and faster. To everyone's surprise, Steve won the final training run. Ken was flying too. An Austrian skier beat them both on the day of the race, but it was hard to be too disappointed. Ken finished second and Steve was third. A young Canadian named Chris Kent was fourth. Ir was fifth, and Mur was seventh. "*A Canadian Tidal Wave*," read the headline in a Swiss newspaper. "The Crazy Canucks are not so crazy," said an Austrian paper.

There were three more races before the Christmas break. The last one was in St.

Moritz, Switzerland. St. Moritz is one of the most famous ski resorts in Europe. It is also one of the oldest. The world's first ski school started there in 1927. The Winter Olympics had been held there in 1928 and 1948.

St. Moritz was steeped in skiing tradition. Its course was narrow and twisting. There were lots of jumps and bumps. It was icy, and it was dangerous. Racers wiped out in training runs the week before the race. During the two final training runs, 21 skiers crashed. That was a World Cup record. Ken bashed his head so hard on a fall that he lost his memory for a few hours. Five racers were hurt so badly they missed the rest of that season. A lot of skiers felt the race should be cancelled. Steve didn't think so. He was actually having fun. He felt he was in complete control. "If I ski well here," Steve realized, "nobody can beat me."

On race day, Steve was nearly perfect. He was strong and steady on his skis, speeding down the hill at an average of 102 kilometres per hour. He was smooth in the turns and on the jumps. No waving arms for balance. No awkward landings on his skis. "They could have made a videotape of his run," said Ken, "and sold it to the rest of us as a training film." No one could catch Steve that day. He set a new course record and earned his first true win on the World Cup circuit. When he went home for Christmas, he was in first place in the standings. "Steve has finally moved to the place where he belongs," Ken said.

The first race after New Year 1981 was at Garmisch-Partenkirchen, Germany. The Garmisch course had lots of flat sections. That was good for gliders, such as Peter Mueller. It was not so good for skiers who liked to bomb down the hill. Not surprisingly, the Crazy Canucks had never done well there. Yet Ken flew down the hill in training. He won both of the last two runs before the race. Steve's best training run was a sixth-place finish.

Steve knew what he had to do in the race. He had to make fast turns in the top section. That would give him enough speed to glide through the flats. Near the bottom, he had to tuck right through a turn in a super fast, icy section called the Gates of Hell. It was never easy to tuck and turn, but Steve went for it. The result was another new course record.

Ken was having a good run too. His time down the hill was right there with Steve's. He might even have beaten him. He certainly would have come in no worse than third. However, Ken fell just a few metres from the finish line. He broke his nose and cut his forehead. There was blood everywhere. Worst of all, he tore the ligaments in his left knee. That injury put him out for the rest of the season.

That night, instead of celebrating his second straight victory, Steve sat with Ken in their hotel room. There was a huge trophy in one corner. There was a pair of crutches in another. Steve brought Ken his supper, and answered questions from all the reporters who phoned them. Then he packed Ken's suitcase for him.

Other Teammates

Over the years, there were always a few other Canadians skiing along with the Crazy Canucks. One of them was Steve's brother, Craig Podborski. Another was Mike Irwin, who was not related to Dave. Others included Gary Aiken, Rob Safrata, Rob Boyd, Chris Kent, Tim Gilhooly, and Robin McLeish. The best of the bunch was Todd Brooker. Brooker and Rob Boyd both won World Cup races during the 1980s.

Steve had always looked to Ken for advice on the hills. Now Ken was going home. Mur and Ir would still be there, but they had not been skiing too well. It would be up to Steve to carry the team. Could he keep on winning without Ken at his side?

11 Fighting to the Finish

Kitzbuhel was the next stop on the 1980–81 World Cup circuit. Ken wouldn't be there to defend the title for Canada. Could Steve do it for him?

Steve had not done very well at Kitzbuhel over the years. "I can remember my first race here," he told reporters. "It scared the bejeepers out of me! I just couldn't believe anyone could ski down it."

Steve had finished 36th back in 1975.

He was nearly seven seconds behind the winner, Franz Klammer. The next year was even worse. That was when he first tore up his knee. Since then, his results had improved. He finished eighth in 1979, but then he crashed again when Ken won in 1980. Still, with two wins in the last two races, Steve was one of the favourites at Kitzbuhel in 1981.

Steve's training runs started off well. He was fast in his first run, and even faster in his second. In fact, he was so fast in his second run that he stood up from his tuck for the last 300 metres — and still won. "I knew I had a great run going," Steve explained. "I wanted the others to think I could win it with my hands tied behind my back."

Perhaps Steve was feeling a bit too sure of himself. That changed the next day when he fell on a training run. "I wasn't hurt," Steve said, "but it knocked the cockiness out of me." He was much slower in his final training run. His skis didn't feel right either. Had he done something to damage them? Steve asked Hans about it. Hans told him the skis were in good shape. "That was enough for me," Steve said. If his equipment was fine, he would just have to ski better.

In the race, Steve launched himself from the start hut and whipped through the first few turns. He hit the first big jump perfectly and sped towards the Steilhang, the steepest part of the course. The right turn through the Steilhang was the hardest turn in ski racing. It was bumpy, and practically dropped off the mountain. Steve rattled into the Steilhang with the wind whistling through his helmet. He had to time the turn perfectly … and he could see that he was running out of room.

Steve was sure he would fly off the

course. He was going to sail into the net, the only thing preventing him from crashing into the trees. He just couldn't let that happen! "Turn, turn, turn," he told himself. "Turn! Turn! Turn!"

Steve struggled to hold his line. When he finally got around the turn, his skis were only inches from the net. He hadn't crashed, but had he lost too much speed? He thought so. "You've just blown it," he told himself.

Steve refused to give up. He dropped back into his tuck and tried to regain speed. He skied the bottom of the course very well, but he was not happy with his run. When he crossed the finish line, he threw his arms up in disgust. He kicked up a huge spray of snow as he stopped, then his body sagged in despair. When he looked up at the clock, he couldn't believe his eyes. His time was nearly a half-second faster than anyone else's! Steve had won his third World Cup race in a row. Nobody but Franz Klammer had done that in the last ten years.

With his quick smile and polite manners, Steve was popular with fans and reporters. He almost never lost his patience when signing autographs or answering questions. The win at Kitzbuhel made him more popular than ever. There were huge celebrations that evening. Everyone seemed happy that Steve had won. Even the Austrian skiers were happy for him. But Peter Mueller wasn't.

Mueller had finished second at Kitzbuhel. It was the second week in a row he was second to Steve. Mueller was also second to Steve in the overall standings. That made Mueller angry.

"Podborski's not the winning type," he growled at journalists. "He's not so good. If I hadn't made three mistakes, I would have won."

Steve just smiled when he heard about Mueller's remarks. "Let me put it this way," he said. "If Mueller was going to win, he wouldn't have made any mistakes."

Mueller got even angrier. He vowed to "send Podborski packing" in the next race at Wengen. The Swiss ace did have a good run there, but he crashed near the bottom. If Mueller had won, he would have tied Steve for first in the standings. Instead, he injured his shoulder. The injury would keep him out of the next few races. That would make it almost impossible for him to win the downhill title again. The battle was down to Steve and a young Austrian named Harti Weirather.

Weirather had been third in the downhill standings for most of the season. With Mueller out, he started closing in on Steve. By the eighth race of the season, their race for the title was a close as it could get.

In addition to his three wins, Steve had finished third in four other races. No one else had reached the podium that many times. However, World Cup rules allowed a skier to count only his five best races. That gave Steve a total of 105 points. Weirather had won just two races, but he had finished second twice. His best five results also gave him 105 points. That meant the whole season would be decided by the final two races at Aspen, Colorado.

Sadly, it was Steve's turn for some bad luck. He had always said ski racing was safer than driving a car. Shortly before the races at Aspen, Steve was driving in the mountains near Whistler, BC. A car that was driving in the wrong lane hit his car nearly head-on. Steve's injuries weren't terrible, but they were pretty serious. They made proper training nearly impossible.

Steve was still pretty sore when he got to Aspen. He finished tenth in the first race, but refused to use his injuries as an excuse. Weirather finished second. Those extra points put him on top of the standings. The only way Steve could be sure of winning the championship was to win the final race.

Steve was the first one on the course that day. At least the forecasted snowstorm didn't reach Aspen. The skies were clear for the final race. The conditions were hard and fast ... just the way the Canadians liked it.

Steve knew what he had to do, and he skied a nearly perfect run. He finished the race with a time of 1:52.49. That was almost two seconds better than he had been the day before. More importantly, it was nearly a half-second faster than the winning time in the first race. Steve had done everything he could on the hill. All he could do after that was wait and see.

Steve's time looked better and better

with each racer who came down the course. Nobody was able to top him. Then, finally, it was Weirather's turn. He, too, skied nearly perfectly. When he was halfway down the course, his time was almost identical to Steve's. Steve was watching the clock and knew it was going to be close. When Weirather crossed the finish line, he fell over. He was exhausted. He didn't move until the announcer called out his time — 1:52.21. He had beaten Steve by 28/100ths of a second. The final standings were 115 points to 110, but Weirather had won the World Cup by less time than it takes to blink an eye!

Steve skied over and gave Weirather a hug. "He deserved it," Steve said. "I didn't lose this race, or the title. Harti won it. I'm proud of what I did. Harti just skied better." For the second year in a row, a Crazy Canuck had come in second. "I won't make any predictions about next season," said Steve. "Only that I'll be trying for something better."

12 Battling All the Best

There were a lot of racers in contention for the downhill title in 1981–82. Steve was certainly one of the favourites. So were Weirather and Mueller. Ken was healthy again. If his knee held up, he had a chance. There was also a surprising name back among the top contenders.

Franz Klammer had not won a race in three years. Suddenly, at the season opener in Val-d'Isère, the Austrian legend was on top again. Back in shape, Klammer could make things tough for everyone.

Ken appeared to have recovered. He finished in fifth place. It was an excellent result for his first race in 11 months. "I feel good," he said. "It's great to be back."

Steve finished fourth. He was fourth again the next week. The season before, he had started the year with two third-place finishes. That meant he was a bit behind his previous pace. At least his 24 points put him ahead of Weirather and Mueller. That was good news. However, Klammer and another Austrian named Erwin Resch were tied for the lead with 34 points.

Steve was anxious to get back to the top of the podium. He did just that in the next race, edging out Mueller by 15/100ths of a second. That put the two rivals 1–2 in the overall standings. Ken finished third in the race, yet both he and Steve felt they could have done better. "I didn't ski brilliantly," Steve admitted, "but I was

good enough to win." He knew he'd have
to ski better after the Christmas break.
Because of bad weather, the first two races
of 1982 were both held at Kitzbuhel. That
was where the season really got
interesting! Weirather hadn't been skiing
well, but that changed quickly. He smashed

*Steve Podborski sits on the shoulders of Peter Mueller
and Ken Read after his first win of the 1981–82
season*

Klammer's old course record to win the first race. Steve and Ken were right behind him in second and third.

Ken and Steve were still roommates, but their relationship had changed. Steve was the team's best skier now. He didn't need Ken's help the way he used to. With Mur and Ir slipping further behind, the Crazy Canucks no longer did everything together. However, teamwork was still important to them. In the second race at Kitzbuhel, Ken was the first Canadian on the course, and he posted another good time. Then he got on the walkie-talkie and radioed his advice to the top of the hill.

"The course is identical to yesterday," Ken said. "It's chopped up in a few places. Plow right through it. Run it like yesterday. Really attack!"

Steve had run into a bit of trouble at the top of the course in the first race. This time, he was much better. But by the bottom, he was going too fast. He almost fell heading into a turn, and then he nearly landed on his back after a jump. Somehow, he managed to slam both skis down beneath him and tuck for the finish line. Ken was waiting for him when he got there. Steve leaped into his arms. The two teammates hugged and exchanged friendly punches. "I let it all hang out," Steve said. "I had a wild run." Steve won the race, and Ken finished third.

Steve now had 94 points in the downhill standings. Ken, Klammer, Weirather, Resch, and Mueller were all tightly bunched behind him. Steve had a big lead, but there were still five races to go. Anything could happen. The race for first place got much tighter the next week when Weirather won at Wengen. Steve finished in 11th place. It was his worst result in two years. Fortunately, he wouldn't have to count those points. His best five results still gave him 94. Weirather was up to 83.

There was just one more race left in Europe. Then, the World Cup season would end with three races in North America. The last race in Europe was at Garmisch in Germany, where Steve had won the year before. This time, Steve broke his own course record and won the race again. His average speed of 108 kilometres an hour was the fastest anyone had been all season.

The World Cup headed to Canada for a race at Whistler, BC. After that, there would be two races in Aspen, Colorado, in the United States. Ken was out of contention, but Steve was in great shape. Steve's point total had increased to 107. One more win in any race would clinch the title. Even without a win, Steve could add points to his total if he finished races in second or third place. The only way for

Klammer, Resch, or Mueller to beat him was if one of them won all three races. And even if Mueller did win all three, Steve could still beat him with just one second-place finish. So, when all the math was figured out, Weirather was the only one with a real chance to beat Steve. Even he would need to win two of the last three races to do it. Anything was possible, but Steve liked his odds.

The weather was perfect for the race at Whistler. It was sunny, but cold. More than 20,000 fans showed up to watch. At that time, it was the biggest crowd ever for a ski race in Canada. Steve could wrap up the World Cup title at home, and the fans were ready to party if he did. "Being in your own country can turn you on," said Steve. "The fans help a lot."

Ironically, the racecourse at Whistler in 1982 was not a good one for Canadian skiers. It was too easy. "Just one long glide from the top to the bottom," was the way Steve described it. The Austrians didn't like it either. "It's too slow," complained Weirather. "It's no good for Steve or me. I don't think he or I will win."

Whistler was the kind of course that Mueller liked. He was the first contender on the mountain on race day, and he did even better than expected. Mueller skied well on the tricky turns at the top and even better on the long glide through the flats. His time was going to be tough for anyone to beat. Weirather certainly didn't. He finished nearly four seconds behind Mueller. Klammer and Resch didn't do much better.

Steve skied much faster than his Austrian rivals. His time was nearly a second slower than Mueller's, but it was still good enough for second place. That meant Mueller, Klammer, and Resch were all out of contention for the downhill title.

Just like in 1981, the battle came down to Steve and Weirather.

This time, Weirather had to win both races in Aspen to beat Steve for the title. It didn't make a difference where Steve finished, and he skied poorly in the first race. So, once again, he had to stand at the bottom and wait for Weirather. The Austrian ace was fast … but not fast enough. When he finished the race in second place, it was official. Steve was the new downhill champion.

"Congratulations," Weirather said to him. "You were the better skier this year."

"It's a very strange feeling," Steve said with a grin. "I feel like I'm in a dream. It's something that's been in our imaginations for so many years. I guess it's come true."

A member of the Canadian men's ski team was finally the World Cup downhill champion. The Crazy Canucks were number one.

Oh, Canada!

Steve was not the only Canadian to do well in front of the home crowd at Whistler. Dave Irwin finished the race in third place. With all his injuries over the years, it was the first time Ir was back on the podium since his win at Schladming in 1975!

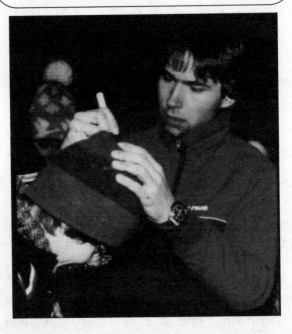

Steve Podborski was always popular with the fans.

Steve Podborski poses with his Fischer skis and the crystal trophy he received for winning the World Cup downhill title in 1982

Epilogue

Today, the name *Crazy Canucks* is a part of Canada's sporting history. Steve Podborski's World Cup title in 1982 was the high point for the team. It also marked the end of an era. Dave Murray and Dave Irwin both decided to retire. The races at Aspen were the last of their World Cup careers.

Steve stayed on for the 1982–83 season. So did Ken Read. Robin McLeish and Todd Brooker joined them on the team. (They had both raced in some World Cup events already.) Todd was a daring skier in the true spirit of the Crazy Canucks. He won two races that winter, including the Hahnenkamm at Kitzbuhel. It was the fourth year in a row that a Canadian won the big race. Not too long before, nobody would have believed that it could happen.

The best that Ken and Steve managed

The Crazy Canucks received a star on Canada's Walk of Fame in 2006.

that winter were some second- and third-place finishes. After the season, Ken decided it was time for him to retire too. "It was fun," he said, "to beat the Europeans at their own game." But after ten years, the fun was gone.

Steve might have retired too, but he had suffered another knee injury. This time it was to his left knee. Since the damage was not too bad, Steve decided to get fit again and try for another comeback. He was in better shape than ever in 1983–84, and he had some good results. He even won another race. But the old desire was no longer there. Steve realized he just didn't want to race anymore. So in 1984 he retired too.

None of the Crazy Canucks were even 30 years old when they left ski racing. They all had to find new careers ... but none of them were ever far from the slopes.

Because he left the team early, people don't usually remember Jim Hunter as one of the Crazy Canucks. After he left the World Cup, Jim had success racing on a professional skiing tour. In 1977–78, he won the first World Pro Downhill title.

After skiing, Jim did television work and sports marketing. Later, he organized the Olympic Torch relay for the Calgary Games. Jim also helps train young athletes, and gives lectures as a motivational speaker.

After 11 top-ten finishes in downhill races, Dave Murray went home to Whistler and became the director of skiing there. He helped run a Canadian racing league for adults, and set up the Dave Murray Summer Ski Camp for children. Sadly, Mur died of cancer on October 23, 1990. He was just 37 years old. In 1991, the top ski run at Whistler was renamed the Dave Murray Downhill — the site of all the men's ski races at the 2010 Winter Olympics.

In his first year of retirement, Dave Irwin coached the New Zealand ski team. He also covered World Cup races on television. Then he became the director of marketing for the Sunshine Village Ski Resort in Banff, Alberta. Later, he even got back into racing. In the late 1990s he skied in a veteran's series with other former World Cup stars.

In 2001, Ir fell during a training run. His head bashed into his knee. It was a fluky accident, but the result was a serious brain injury. Ir was in a coma for four days. When he woke up, he couldn't remember anything. He couldn't recognize his father or his children. He didn't even know who he was. He was like an infant. He couldn't do anything by himself. Ir spent the next three months in hospital. He spent even longer doing therapy and exercises. Many people who suffer brain injuries don't survive. Just one year after his accident, Ir was back on his skis. He knew he was one of the lucky ones. In order to help others, he and his family set up the Dave Irwin Foundation for Brain Injury.

Steve and Ken did not have to face the hardships that the two Daves faced. After Steve retired from racing, he worked with a sportswear company. He had his own line of ski clothes and did a lot of work on television. He worked on the bid that brought the 2010 Winter Olympics to Vancouver and Whistler. Now he is the director of sports marketing for a tele-communications company. His company sponsors major sports events and donates money to Canadian athletes, including the ski team.

Ken spent 14 years as a skiing analyst on TV. He also ran his own sports marketing company. In 1988, Ken carried the Olympic flame into the stadium when the Winter Olympics were held in Calgary.

From 2002 to 2008, Ken was the head of Alpine Canada Alpin. That's the organization that runs ski racing in Canada. Canadian skiers had not been doing well when Ken took over, but he brought a new attitude to the program. Or, maybe, he brought an old one. "Our goal is to WIN," he said. "We want to return Canadian athletes to the podium. Our mission is to be best in the world at every level."

With Ken in charge and Steve helping to raise funds, Canada's men's and women's ski teams once again became a threat to win any race they entered … just like they were in the heyday of the Crazy Canucks.

Glossary

Alpine/Alpine skiing: A term relating to high mountains. Alpine originally referred to the Alps, a mountain range in Europe. Alpine skiing means skiing down a mountain, either in a race or just for enjoyment.

Amateur: A person who is not paid money to do something, such as compete in a sport.

Canuck: A slang term meaning a Canadian.

Chalet: A word for a type of cabin or cottage originally built in Switzerland. Many ski resorts all over the world refer to their buildings as chalets.

Compression: A squeezing of something to make it smaller. In downhill ski racing, compression is the feeling of being squished in on yourself as you flatten out after a steep drop or tight turn.

Concussion: An injury to the brain, usually caused by a blow to the head.

Downhill: The term "downhill skiing" is often used to mean Alpine skiing. In racing, downhill is the fastest type of race, and therefore the most dangerous.

Nordic/Nordic skiing: A term relating to the northwestern countries of Europe, particularly Norway, Sweden, and Finland. Nordic skiing is any type of skiing in which the heel of the boot is not attached to the ski, such as cross-country skiing and ski jumping.

Podium: A small, raised platform. In many sports, the top three finishers receive their trophies or medals while standing on a podium.

Professional: A person who is paid money to do a job or compete in a sport.

Rookie: Somebody who is new to an activity or job. In sports, a rookie is a person who is in their first year.

Slalom/Giant slalom: A ski race on a zigzag course where racers have to make tight turns around flags on poles. The giant slalom is a longer race than the slalom, and the turns are not as tight. Slalom and giant slalom races have always been a part of the World Cup ski circuit, along with the downhill.

Sponsor: In sports, a sponsor is a person or a company who provides money to help support a team, an athlete, or an event.

Start hut: A small building at the top of the course where the skiers begin their race. Skiers start the race by going through an opening no bigger than a regular-sized door. The opening has a small gate with an electronic wire that starts the clock that times their race.

Super G: Super G is short for Super Giant Slalom. It is a race that combines aspects of the downhill and the giant slalom. The Super G was introduced to the World Cup circuit in 1982.

Tuck: In ski racing, a tuck is a deep crouch, with knees bent low and back arching forward. This position allows a skier to cut through the wind more easily and go as fast as possible.

Veteran: Somebody who has a lot of experience in an activity, or has played a sport for a long time.

Walkie-talkie: A hand-held, two-way radio used by people to talk to each other over a distance.

World Cup: A sports tournament in which teams from many different countries take part. The first World Cup was held for soccer in 1930. Since the start of the World Cup ski circuit in 1966, there have been World Cup events in many different sports.

Acknowledgements

Writing about sports history, I don't get too many chances to write about people I actually got to watch. With the Crazy Canucks, I didn't just watch them ... I wanted to be one of them! For me, though, writing this book is as close as I ever got to racing on the World Cup ski circuit.

With the time difference overseas, it was often hard to follow the Crazy Canucks. Races at noon in Europe were already over by 5:00 or 6:00 a.m. where I lived in Toronto. Did I want to listen to the sports news on the radio as soon as I woke up? Or did I want to wait until the CBC showed the race on TV that afternoon? It was always more exciting to watch a race when you didn't know what happened ... but I usually couldn't wait that long to find out how the Crazy Canucks had done that day. My mom let me miss school to watch the downhill at the 1980 Lake Placid Olympics live on TV. That night, my brothers and I called the Podborski house in Don Mills to offer our congratulations!

I could not possibly have written this book without the autobiographies written by Steve Podborski (with Gerald Donaldson) and Ken Read (with Matthew Fisher). E-mailing back and forth with Ken Read while writing this book has been a real thrill for me, and I certainly hope it wasn't too much of a bother for him. Thank you so much, Ken, for your thoughtful answers. Thank you also to my wife Barbara for suggesting I write about the Crazy Canucks, to Lynne Harrison, and to Faye Smailes, Allison McDonald, and Kat Mototsune at Lorimer for all of their help.

About the Author

ERIC ZWEIG is a managing editor with Dan Diamond and Associates, consulting publishers to the NHL. He has written about sports and sports history for many major publications, including the *Toronto Star* and *The Globe and Mail*. He has also been a writer/producer with CBC Radio Sports and TSN SportsRadio, and written several popular books about hockey for both adults and children. He lives in Owen Sound, Ontario, with his family.

Photo Credits

We gratefully acknowledge the following sources for permission to reproduce the images within this book.

BC Sports Hall of Fame and Museum: p 32, p 70, back cover bottom
Canada's Sports Hall of Fame: p 63
Craigleith Ski Club: p 96, p 126, p 127
James Lorimer & Company Ltd., Publishers: p 129
Ken Read Private Collection: p 26, p 29, p 49, p 50, p 57, p 68, p 82, p 119, front cover top, front cover bottom, back cover top, back cover middle
Kitzbuhel Ski Club: p 10